Tasmanian Quest

marion & steve isham

to
Anne, Susan and Kate
at
Oz for Kids
whose questing
is an inspiration

Bandicoot
BOOKS
pages to be rapt in

I know a child
– born by my mother

natural born as any other
that is neither my
sister nor brother

ong ago, on a far away island lived Marreena.
Her village of Stan Lea nestled against a great rock rising
out of the sea.

Marreena was a fisherman's daughter.

As Marreena pulled in the nets one evening,
an old flounder begged to be released.

"I can help you," he said.
"The fisherfolk drag
in their nets
and each day
there are fewer fish."
Marreena knew
this to be true.
For many weeks
an enchantment
had brought hunger
to the village.

"What must be done?" asked Marreena.

"Take the sword from the great rock.
Your courage will break the spell
and that sword will serve you well."

Then he vanished into the dark sea.

Next morning Marreena climbed the Rock with Tyga, her companion from childhood.   The sword of which the flounder spoke had been stuck fast for as long as anyone could remember. On that day everything would change. Clasping the sword, Marreena pulled it free with the ease of young Arthur in the legend.

Down in the village the people marveled. Then Marreena's father spoke for all to hear. He was a wise man and knew there was more to the world than the land, the sea and the sky above.

"Marreena," he said, "you know we live from the sea and would starve, but for our fisherfolk and their nets. Inquire the advice of the old woman of West Bree. She will understand the flounder's words."

So Marreena set out on a journey.

Though the way was long, canny Tyga brought Marreena by sure
paths to the village of West Bree and the cottage of the old woman.

Speaking kindly, the old woman unrolled a map.
"Your path leads on from my door to places you have never seen."
And she told Marreena much of the way ahead.

"Bring me one flower from the world's oldest plant
but beware great danger.

       Your courage will break the spell
        and this journey will serve you well."

Then the old woman gave Marreena a tightly woven basket.
"Fill this at the Falls of Saint Columba, my dear."

At the Falls, try as she would,
Marreena's basket would hold no water.
"Fill it this time for me," said Grey Kangaroo,
with the voice of an old man.
And as Marreena carried it to him
not a drop escaped.

Once again Marreena filled her basket
and followed her map to the south.

No sooner had she set foot on the
Spiked Bridge when there emerged
from below a great Troll-devil who
snarled and threatened and would
not let her pass. Tyga's hackles rose
and he would have rushed the creature.

But Marreena, in a sudden impulse splashed
the contents of her basket at the menacing
eyes and slathering jaws. And the magic
of the water shrank the creature to little
more than a pup. Screeching, it retreated,
and was never seen in its old shape again.

At length Marreena arrived in the city.
Strolling through the market she took pity on
a cage of birds, offering her basket in exchange.

Few think of me
enough they've got
but all can tell
when they have no...

She carried them to the Tower of Arthur where she climbed to the battlements and there released them.

The sorrow of that place was lifted and a gentle peace settled all about.

And Marreena
travelled on.

Marreena's path led up the Mountain where she read
runes on ancient stones. At last she understood the
task that lay before her.

Marreena was afraid and thought of turning back.
Then she read:

"Your courage will break the spell
and these words will serve you well."

Then came Marreena's darkest hour. Deep in the forest a loathsome dragon entwined the oldest plant in all the world. One flower must Marreena pluck and take to the old woman.

The dragon fixed his eyes
on the intrepid girl.
A fresh victim had come
his way, but for the
moment he would play.
"What can one so small and
weak bring against one so
deadly and so dread?"
he mocked, his smoky
voice full of malice.

But Marreena
answered in
riddles for she
had learned on
the mountain
that this was a
riddling dragon.

"Three weapons have I here," she cried,
"and each lies within the others!

We're treasured up
We're thrown away
We're made to sting
We're made to play

My face is smooth and shining bright
which mostly I keep out of sight
within my house.
Here I lie snug, unless in anger,
I look out sharp, suspecting danger."

Beguiled, his dragon lids dropped in thought
over flinty eyes and Marreena seized her moment.

With both hands she drove her sword deep and
Tyga sprang to his throat tearing dragon flesh
so that dark dragon blood came from the wounds.

With choking cry he leapt high in the air.
Then fell like a stone into the Southern Sea.
And fishes there now swim among his bones.

So Marreena took a flower of King's Holly, for that was the plant's name, and Tyga carried her back to West Bree.

icebergs here

whales here

dragons were here

penguins and seals here

tower of arthur

the city

ancient rune stone

mountains

spiked bridge

old as the hills but always new a carpet dyed with every hue

west ruins

harbour

here are tigers

falls of st columba

west bree

forester kangaroos here

scan lea

the great rock

schools of fish here

The old woman gratefully received the flower.
It was wondrous medicine and cured her failing sight.
"Go now," she said, "and return to your home,
for what you have sought has been given."

The streets of Stan Lea were filled with celebration.
A girl's courage had indeed ended the enchantment
for now there was enough to eat and more.